The Princes
and
The Treasure

Jeffrey A. Miles
Illustrated by J. L. Phillips

Handsome
Prince
Publishing
HandsomePrincePublishing.com

Dedicated to my handsome prince, Patrick Lastowski.
Thank you for all your love, support, encouragement, and wisdom.
May we live happily ever after.

— Jeffrey Miles

The Princes and The Treasure

Once upon a time, there was a magical kingdom named Evergreen. The ruler of Evergreen was King Rufus. He was a stern king, who was always shouting orders.

King Rufus had a beautiful daughter named Princess Elena. The princess always honored and obeyed her father, until one day when she and the king took a walk in the park.

"It's time you found a husband," said the king.

"But I'm not ready for a husband!" cried the princess.

Suddenly, an old woman
whisked away the princess in a
carriage.
"Stop!" yelled King Rufus.
"Bring back my daughter!"
But the carriage was already
out of sight.

The king was heartsick that his beautiful daughter was missing. He called all the townspeople together and made a big announcement.

"Whoever saves Princess Elena may marry her," declared the king.

The strongest man in Evergreen was named Gallant. He loved to compete, because he won every challenge. He was handsome, and dashing, and the most desired man in town. Many people tried to attract his attention, but no one succeeded.

"I'll save the princess," boasted Gallant.

In a nearby village, lived a young man named Earnest. He was quiet, and shy, and preferred happy endings. He loved a great adventure, but only those in books.

"Why don't you stop reading, and go help the princess," said Earnest's mother.

"But I can't save the princess," said Earnest.

"Yes, you can," she replied. "Now go!"

So Earnest sadly left his cozy, little cottage, and he went to save the princess.

Earnest followed the trail of the carriage to a dark tower. A strong young man was already there.

"I'm Gallant," said the young man. "Who are you?"

"Uh, I'm Earnest," said Earnest softly.

The old woman suddenly appeared.

"Release the princess," demanded Gallant.

"You may take the princess, if you bring me the greatest treasure in the land," said the old woman. "You must bring me the earth, the wind, the sun, the moon, and the stars."

Then the old woman vanished.

"How do we find the greatest treasure in the land?" wondered Gallant.

"Let's ask the Oracle," said Earnest. "She's very wise. She'll know what to do."

"Earnest isn't very strong," thought Gallant to himself. "But he's smart. I'd better keep an eye on him."

Gallant and Earnest ran to the temple of the Oracle.

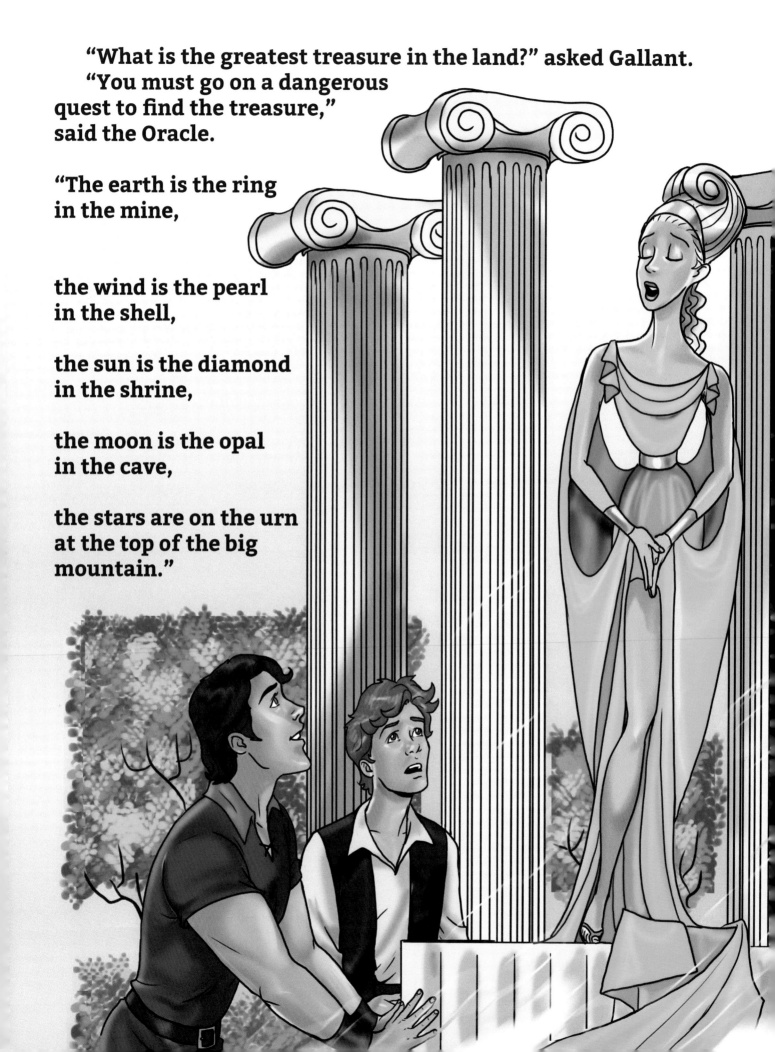

"What is the greatest treasure in the land?" asked Gallant.
"You must go on a dangerous quest to find the treasure," said the Oracle.

"The earth is the ring in the mine,

the wind is the pearl in the shell,

the sun is the diamond in the shrine,

the moon is the opal in the cave,

the stars are on the urn at the top of the big mountain."

Gallant ran to the mine ahead of Earnest. A huge grizzly bear blocked the entrance. Gallant fought the bear with all his might, but he wasn't strong enough. Gallant had to run away without the ring.

"Bears like honey," thought Earnest. "I'll find a beehive and get some honey for the bear."

Earnest tried to scoop some honey out of a hive, but bees flew out of the hive and stung him.

Earnest made some grass smoke and calmed the bees. He grabbed some honeycomb and set it near the mine. The bear smelled the honeycomb, and went to get the honey. Earnest ran into the mine and grabbed the ring.

"I did it!" cried Earnest.

"I can't believe that bookworm got the ring," thought Gallant.

Gallant swam down to the shoal, but a huge octopus guarded the shell. Gallant tried to swim past the octopus, but the octopus grabbed him. Gallant twisted out of the strong arms, and he was able to get the pearl.

"I beat you this time, Earnest," thought Gallant.

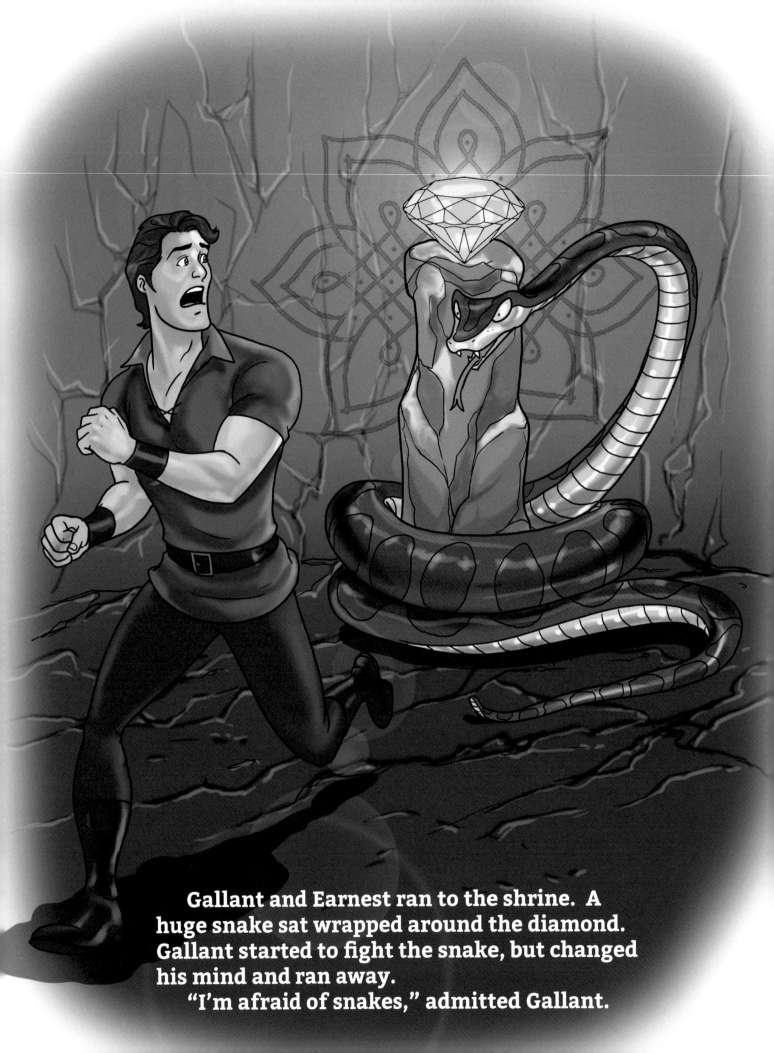

Gallant and Earnest ran to the shrine. A huge snake sat wrapped around the diamond. Gallant started to fight the snake, but changed his mind and ran away.

"I'm afraid of snakes," admitted Gallant.

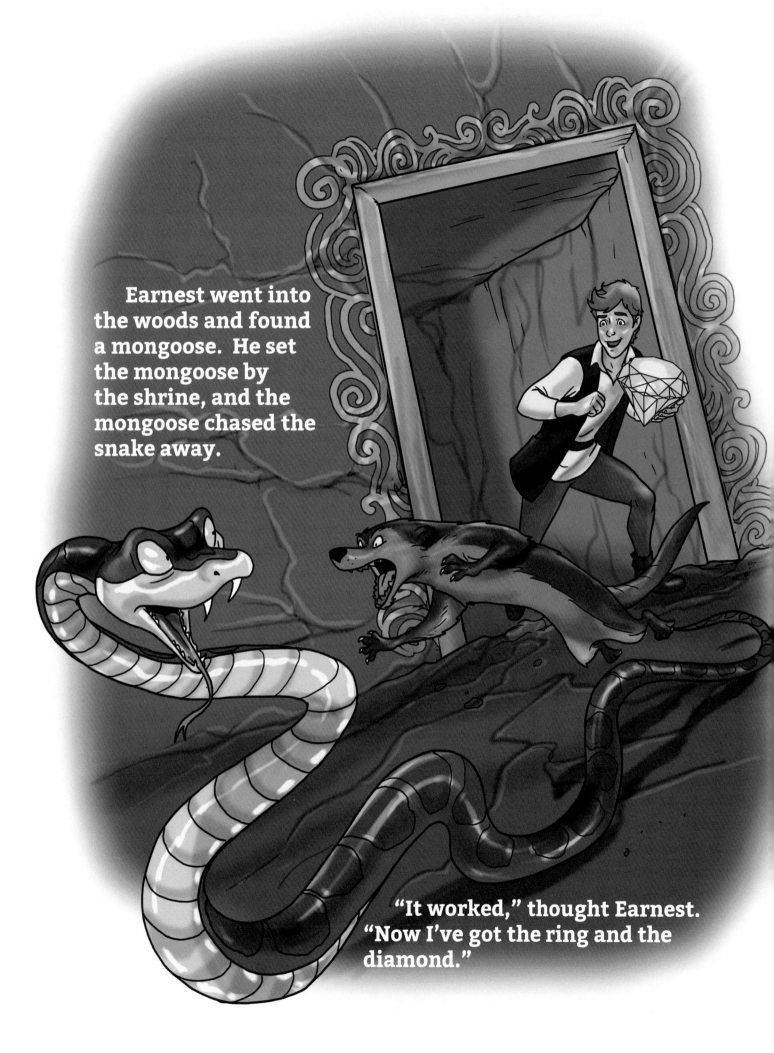

Earnest went into the woods and found a mongoose. He set the mongoose by the shrine, and the mongoose chased the snake away.

"It worked," thought Earnest. "Now I've got the ring and the diamond."

Gallant and Earnest walked to the cave to get the opal, but a giant wolf guarded the entrance.
"One of us will have to run near the wolf so the wolf chases him," said Gallant.

"I'm good at hiding," said Earnest. "I'll run by the wolf, then I'll hide when he chases me."

The wolf chased Earnest, and Gallant grabbed the opal.
"You were great," said Gallant, admiring Earnest.

After a long search, Earnest and Gallant found the big mountain where the urn with the stars was hidden.

"Race you to the top," shouted Gallant as he ran up the mountain.

"There's no way I can run up there," thought Earnest.

Earnest found a goat and rode it up the mountain. He got to the top before Gallant.

Earnest wasn't able to pick up the urn.
"Let me try," said Gallant, but he couldn't lift it either.
"We have to do it together," said Earnest, smiling at Gallant.
Earnest and Gallant both grabbed a handle and lifted the urn.
"The Oracle was wrong," said Earnest.
"I know," replied Gallant.
"The greatest treasure in the land is finding each other!" they both shouted.

Gallant and Earnest went back to the dark tower.

"Did you bring what I asked?" shrieked the old woman.

"Yes," they both said. "We brought you the greatest treasure in the land."

Earnest and Gallant looked at each other.

Gallant said, "Earnest is my earth, my wind, my sun, my moon, and my stars."

Earnest said, "Gallant is my earth, my wind, my sun, my moon, and my stars."

Upon hearing this news, the old woman transformed into a beautiful enchantress.

"True love is the greatest treasure of all," said the enchantress. "You were not finding each other on your own. So I created this quest to bring you two together."

The doors to the tower opened and Princess Elena emerged.
"You're free!" cried Earnest and Gallant.
"I wasn't a prisoner," said the princess. "I made a wish that
I wouldn't have to marry a prince, and the enchantress made
my wish come true."
"We're so glad you're safe and sound," said Gallant.

Earnest, Gallant, and Princess Elena went to see King Rufus. "Earnest and Gallant, your strength and bravery shall be rewarded," said the king. "I name you Prince Gallant. I name you Prince Earnest. Which one of you will marry the princess?"

"We don't want to marry the princess," admitted Earnest and Gallant. "We want to marry each other."

Earnest and Gallant invited all their family and friends to their wedding.

"I now pronounce you married," said the Vicar. "May you love each other forever."

"Oh, Earnest has never looked happier," sighed Earnest's mother.

King Rufus was pleased his daughter was happy and safe. He gave Earnest and Gallant a bag of gold and lots of land. The two princes worked very hard and built a castle of their own.

In the main room of their castle, Gallant and Earnest built a huge fireplace. They put the ring, the pearl, the diamond, the opal, and the urn on its great mantle.

"These remind me that we had to work together to find each other," said Gallant.

"They remind me that you are my earth, my wind, my sun, my moon, and my stars," said Earnest smiling at Gallant.

"And you are my earth, my wind, my sun, my moon, and my stars," said Gallant smiling at Earnest.

Earnest and Gallant stood in front of their new home
and admired all their hard work.
"What a beautiful castle," said Earnest.
"We're going to be very happy here," said Gallant.
"Yes, we are," sighed Earnest.

And the two princes lived happily ever after.

CPSIA information can be obtained
at www.ICGtesting.com
Printed in the USA
LVIC05n2256230414
383020LV00011B/43

9 780099 105363 6